KT-525-220

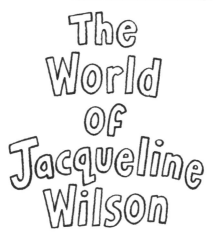

The World of Jacqueline Wilson

www.jacquelinewilson.co.uk

When I was a little girl people went in for dressmaking in a big way. You used to be able to buy huge pattern books filled with hundreds of drawings of women and children wearing shirtwaister frocks and dinky dresses. I always saved up my pocket money to buy these pattern books. I wasn't into dressmaking. I could barely sew on a button. No, I wanted pattern books so I could cut out all the people and play elaborate imaginary games with them. The paper pattern men just wore dressing gowns and looked a bit silly and there were hardly any boys, but I was content playing with the ladies and the little girls. (Maybe that's why there aren't many boys in my books!) I kept them in a big cardboard box and I crayonned on the top MY WORLD.

I made up many stories about those paper people. I haven't changed much now, because I'm *still* making up stories, filling my books with imaginary children. But although I make them all up, they're very real to me. I hope you enjoy reading about their families and friends, their pets, their fears and wishes, their schooldays and special days.

I've added little pieces about myself to introduce each section and there's a place for you to write about your-self too. I hope you have fun in the World of Jacqueline Wilson!

Jacqueline Wilson

Also available by Jacqueline Wilson:

Published in Young Corgi, for newly confident readers:

LIZZIE ZIPMOUTH
SLEEPOVERS

Available from Doubleday/Corgi Yearling Books:

BAD GIRLS
THE BED & BREAKFAST STAR
BEST FRIENDS
BURIED ALIVE!
THE CAT MUMMY
CLEAN BREAK
CLIFFHANGER
THE DARE GAME
DOUBLE ACT
GLUBBSLYME
THE ILLUSTRATED MUM
LOLA ROSE
THE LOTTIE PROJECT
MIDNIGHT
THE MUM-MINDER
SECRETS
THE STORY OF TRACY BEAKER
THE SUITCASE KID
VICKY ANGEL
THE WORRY WEBSITE

The World of Jacqueline Wilson

Jacqueline Wilson
Illustrated by Nick Sharratt

DOUBLEDAY

THE WORLD OF JACQUELINE WILSON
A DOUBLEDAY BOOK 0385 60888 8

Published in Great Britain in 2005 by Doubleday,
an imprint of Random House Children's Books

1 3 5 7 9 10 8 6 4 2

Compiled by Kelly Cauldwell

RANDOM HOUSE CHILDREN'S BOOKS
61–63 Uxbridge Rd, London W5 5SA
A division of The Random House Group Ltd

RANDOM HOUSE AUSTRALIA (PTY) LTD
20 Alfred Street, Milsons Point, Sydney,
New South Wales 2061, Australia

RANDOM HOUSE NEW ZEALAND LTD
18 Poland Road, Glenfield, Auckland 10, New Zealand

RANDOM HOUSE (PTY) LTD
Endulini, 5A Jubilee Road, Parktown 2193, South Africa

THE RANDOM HOUSE GROUP Limited Reg. No. 954009
www.kidsatrandomhouse.co.uk

A CIP catalogue record for this book is available from the British Library.

Printed and bound in Singapore

Friends

Friends

by

Jacqueline Wilson

I had lots of friends when I was at primary school but I didn't have a *best* friend. I also had imaginary friends when I was little. I used to mutter to them when I was walking along the road. People probably thought I was seriously loopy!

I didn't know anyone the first rather scary day at my secondary school. There was a friendly-looking girl with plaits sitting in front of me. When the bell went and we were told to go to the art room, I timidly tapped her on the back and asked if she knew the way. She didn't have a clue either but we went off in search of it together. Chris and I became best friends that day, and we're *still* best friends many years later.

She drew a funny, podgy, little girl with lots of yellow hair. I wasn't sure whether I was pleased or not. She saw me hesitating, so she drew me special strappy high-heeled clunky sandals on my feet. She drew a line of blue sky at the top of the page, and then right above my head she did a big yellow sun with rays all around it. Then she wrote a title at the top. Her writing was rather wobbly and I knew she'd spelled a word wrong but it didn't matter a bit. MY FREND MANDY. That's what she wrote. And I felt so happy I felt as if there was a real sun above my head and I was dancing in its warm yellow rays.

MANDY
Bad Girls

I wish Maria was my friend but she's Alice's best friend. *Everyone* in my class has got a best friend - or else they go around in little gangs like Lucy and Imogen and Sarah and Claudia. It's so awful not having a gang, not having a best friend. I *used* to. I used to have Miranda... Miranda could be a bit boring sometimes because she never had any ideas of her own - but I always had *heaps* of ideas so I suppose it didn't matter too much. Miranda wasn't much use at playing pretend games but at least she didn't laugh at me.

INDIA
Secrets

I'd had a nightmare about my mum and it had brought on a bad attack of my hay fever. Normally I like to keep to myself at such moments as some stupid ignorant twits think my red eyes and runny nose are because I've been crying. And I never ever cry, no matter what. But I knew Peter wouldn't tease me so I huddled down beside him for a bit and when I felt him shivering I put my arm around him and told him he was quite possibly my best friend ever.

TRACY
The Story of Tracy Beaker

I liked Emily *soooo* much. I wished she could be my best friend. But she already had Chloe for her best friend. I didn't think much of Chloe. I liked Amy and Bella though. We'd started to go around in this little bunch of five, Amy and Bella and Emily and Chloe and me. We formed this special secret club. We called ourselves the Alphabet Girls. It's because of our names. I'm Daisy. So our first names start with A B C D and E. I was the one who spotted this. The secret club was all my idea too.

DAISY
Sleepovers

I was so enchanted by my sudden astonishing friendship with Jasmine that I didn't even want to think about Will. Jasmine and I whispered and wrote notes

all through lessons and walked round arm in arm together at lunch time. Jasmine linked her arm through mine as if it was the most natural thing in the world. I'd been friends with Marnie and Terry for more than a year and we'd never linked arms once. Marnie and Terry disapproved of girls who went round cosied up together and called them stupid names.

VIOLET
Midnight

Arthur King was waiting at the bus stop. I stared at him instead. He was reading a book. He was always reading books. I like reading too. It was shame Arthur King was a boy. And a bit weird. Otherwise we might have been friends. I didn't have any proper friends now. I used to have Melanie but then she got friendly with Sarah. Then Kim decided she'd have them in her gang.

MANDY
Bad Girls

Lisa   Me   Angela

I don't want to sound disgustingly boastful but I'm the one Angela and Lisa are desperate to sit next to. Lots of the girls want to be best friends with me, actually. I'm just best friends with Lisa and Angela, but anyone can be in our special Girls' Gang. Any girl. No boys allowed. That goes without saying. Even though I just did.

CHARLIE
The Lottie Project

I'd never been very good at making friends. I had a special friend way back in Year One at Keithstone Primary, a little girl called Diana who had bunches tied with pink bobbles and a Minnie Mouse doll. We sat together and shared wax crayons and plastic scissors and we played skipping in the playground together and we visited the

scary smelly toilets together too, waiting outside the door for each other. But then we moved, we were always moving in those days, sometimes several times a year and I never found another Diana.

DOLPHIN
The Illustrated Mum

Sometimes Aileen and her mum would come back to Mulberry Cottage with us and we'd have fruit juice – once we had *mulberry* juice – and Aileen and I would play Sylvanian Families. . . I still see Aileen every day at school but it's not the same any more.. Aileen's mum gives a lift home to Fiona now. Aileen and Fiona play together after school. We go round in this sort of three-some at playtime. Aileen keeps insisting she's still my friend but when we have

to join up with a partner in class now she always goes with Fiona.

is for Friends

ANDY
The Suitcase Kid

Vicky's my best friend. We're closer than sisters. They call us The Twins at school because we're so inseparable. We've been best friends ever since we were at nursery school together and I crept up to Vicky at the water trough and she pulled a funny face and then tipped her red plastic teapot and started watering me. . . We're going to be best friends for ever and ever and ever, through school, through college, through work. It doesn't matter about falling in love. Vicky's had loads of boyfriends but no one can ever mean as much to us as each other.

JADE
Vicky Angel

I wanted to stay with Jasmine but I didn't want her to feel she was lumbered with me all the time. Maybe she was dying to make friends with some of the other girls. She didn't belong with me. She could be friends with anyone, Alicia, Gemma, Aisling, Lucy, all the pretty cool clever girls with designer clothes and boyfriends.

VIOLET
Midnight

I sometimes go around in the gang, though I can't stick Brian. Actually, Blob isn't too keen on him either. So we've started going around together. Just me and him. He still calls me Baldie. I still call him Blob. But it doesn't matter because we're mates. It's great to have someone to pal around with. Someone different, not someone the same as me.

RUBY
Double Act

My Friends

School

by

Jacqueline Wilson

We had very eccentric teachers at my primary school. There was one lady called Miss Audric who had very long ginger hair coiled up in plaits and wore hand-knitted purple suits. She taught us Nature Study and once took us for a seven-mile walk in Richmond Park. We were all on our knees by the time we

got back to school. My favourite teacher was Mr Townsend who was very kind and gentle and loved art. I loved art too, and I enjoyed the Art lessons at my secondary school, taught by a delightfully funny and talented Polish Count. I also liked my English lessons, although Miss Pierce was forever outlining words in red ink and writing 'Slang!' in the margin. I bet she'd outline half the text in my books now!

I was very very very bad at Maths and totally useless when it came to Games and I couldn't catch a ball. I'm so glad I never have to play another game of netball, hockey or rounders in my life!

It's awful. We knew it would be. It's like a little toy school. There's hardly any playground. There aren't any computers. There isn't even a television. The teacher writes stuff up on the blackboard and we sit at these dinky little desks with lids and inkwells. It's like the sort of classroom you get in a cartoon.

RUBY
Double Act

Sometimes the teachers like me. Sometimes they don't. They called me Miss-Know-It-All at my last school. I heard them discussing me in the staffroom. This new teacher Miss Strand thinks I'm thick. She tells me stuff very *s-l-o-w-l-y* and she keeps saying I mustn't worry if I can't do the work. It's a wonder she hasn't stuck me at the back like the kids with learning difficulties.

TREASURE
Secrets

I'm good at imagining. Whenever we have History and we have to imagine what it would feel like to be a Roman centurion or a Tudor queen or a London child in the Blitz I can always pretend I'm there and I can write it all down and Mrs Hunter gives me excellent marks. Even though I'm imagining so hard I forget about paragraphs and punctuation and my spelling goes all to pot.

APRIL
Dustbin Baby

When we were all new girls in Year Seven we'd been asked to describe our homes for an English lesson. I was stupid enough to be truthful. Mrs Mason, our English teacher, made me read my essay out loud. I had to tell the whole class about the Rose Fairy and the Crow Fairy and all the other fairy-folk. They all started snorting with laughter and flapping their arms in mock flight. I tried reading with Will-irony, one eyebrow raised, to show I knew it was ridiculous to have fairies flitting from your ceiling but it was too late. I might be cool Will's sister but I was clearly the saddest little baby in Year Seven.

VIOLET
Midnight

'If someone is being bullied you should always tell', said Miss Moseley, her eyes swivelling round the whole circle. 'Tell your mum and dad. Tell your teacher. Tell another teacher if things still don't get sorted out. The person who is getting bullied needs help. And the people doing the bullying need help too, because they're sad, sick, silly people. We should feel sorry for them, even though they hurt and do a lot of harm. Even name-calling and silly teasing can be horribly upsetting, can't it?' She looked around the circle again.

MANDY
Bad Girls

Then he told us about all the food they had for school dinners when he was a little boy. You had disgusting things like smelly stew all glistening with fat and grey mince that looked as if someone had chewed it all up. You had cabbage like old seaweed and lumpy mashed potato and tinned peas that smelt like feet. 'But we ate it all up because if you didn't you weren't allowed to have pudding. Puddings were the whole point of school dinners. We had jam roly-poly and bread-and-butter pudding and chocolate sponge with chocolate sauce and apple pie and custard and absolute best of all, trifle'.

WILLIAM
The Worry Website

So now school's a doddle. Because Garnet and I don't do anything. We just sit looking blank when Dumbo Debenham gets on to us. Or I write the barest minimum and Garnet does mirror-writing. Or we copy everything twice. . . two lots of sums, two maps, two fact-sheets, because we say everything's got to be doubled because we're a double ourselves. 'Double trouble,' says Dumbo Debenham.

RUBY
Double Act

It had been the one ultra big bonus of life at the Oyal Htl. NO SCHOOL. I knew Naomi and Funny-Face and most of the other kids at the hotel had to go. I'd hoped I'd not got noticed. I don't like school. Well, my first school was OK. There was a smiley teacher and we could play with pink dough and we all got to sing these soppy old nursery rhymes. I could sing loudest and longest.

ELSA
The Bed and Breakfast Star

Miss Beckworth. She was new so I thought she'd be young. When you get a new young teacher they're often ever so

Miss Beckworth

strict the first few weeks just to show you who's boss, and then they relax and get all friendly. Then you can muck about and do whatever you want. I *love* mucking about, doing daft things and making everyone laugh. Even the teachers. But the moment I set eyes on Miss Beckworth I knew none of us were going to be laughing.

CHARLIE
The Lottie Project

Miranda goes to boarding school now. She *wanted* to go. She loves the *Harry Potter* books and thought the whole boarding school idea would be wonderful – but she positively hated it at first. She wept buckets – tanks – a whole *swimming pool*. The letter she wrote to me was all tear-stained and smudgy. . . I would hate to go to boarding school because I'm sure I wouldn't fit in. You have to play team games and I'd never get picked.

INDIA
Secrets

I trudged on towards Holybrook Primary. Nearly everyone got taken by their mothers, even the kids in Year Six. Marigold hardly ever took me to school. Mostly she stayed in bed in the morning. I didn't mind. It was easier that way. I didn't like to think about the times when she *had* come to school, when she'd gone right in and talked to the teachers. I ran to stop myself thinking and touched the school gate seven times for luck. It didn't work. We had to divide up into partners for letter-writing and no one wanted to be my partner.

DOLPHIN
The Illustrated Mum

11

It's time to go home now but we're checking out this big notice on the cloakroom door about after-school clubs. We've got a brand new head teacher who's fussed because Downfield is considered a bit of a dump and so he's determined we're all going to do better in our exams and get involved with all these extra-curricular activities.

'It's bad enough having to go to school,' Vicky says. 'So who's sad enough to want to stay *after* – like, voluntarily?'

I nod out of habit. I always agree with Vicky. But I've just read a piece about a new drama club and I can't help feeling wistful.

JADE
Vicky Angel

My School

Special Occasions
by
Jacqueline Wilson

I never had any big parties when I was a child because we lived in a small flat and there wasn't room. I don't give big parties now, because I live in a tiny house and there *certainly* isn't room. I have a vast collection of 15,000 books in higgledy-piggledy piles reaching right up to the ceiling. I can only entertain my friends one at a time!

However, my lovely publishers recently threw a wonderful party for me at the *Ritz* to celebrate my books selling ten million copies. We all had champagne and delicious canapes and everyone talked at the tops of their voices and had a great time . . . especially me! I was given a great big bunch of flowers, a beautiful box of chocolates and a very special silver and quartz hand-made ring.

We had this BIG New Year's Eve party last night and I couldn't believe the number of people who were squashed up in the flat at twelve o'clock. It was just like the tube in rush hour, only there everyone has glum faces and keeps quiet, whereas here everyone was happy, happy, happy, bouncing about and laughing and drinking and dancing. I got to stay up too – and Patsy. Even little Britney made it past midnight.

TREASURE
Secrets

We did this special dance over and over until we all knew it backwards (though Bella still *faced* backwards if you didn't watch her). The we performed it like a real girl group to Amy's mum and her dad and her nan and they all clapped and clapped and said we were great. Then we had our tea and there was the chocolate cake Amy had promised. It was chocolate sponge inside with three layers of chocolate cream and there were even little chocolate drops all around the frosted chocolate icing on top of the cake.

DAISY
Sleepovers

Marigold started going weird again on her birthday. Star remembered that birthdays were often bad times so we'd tried really hard. Star made her a beautiful

big card cut into the shape of a marigold. She used up all the ink in the orange felt-tip colouring it in. Then she did two sparkly silver threes with her special glitter pen and added 'Happy Birthday' in her best italic writing. They do Calligraphy in Year Eight and she's very good at it.

DOLPHIN
The Illustrated Mum

She let me choose this amazing dark red for our bedroom, and we've got these truly wonderful crimson curtains we found at a boot fair and a deep purply-red lamp and when it's a treat day like a birthday we draw the curtains and switch on the lamp and have a special red picnic in our beautifully bright bedroom. Cherries, plums, jam tarts, strawberry split ice creams, Ribena for me and red wine for Jo, yum yum.

CHARLIE
The Lottie Project

Bella's mum had her birthday tea all ready for us. It was a HUGE tea. There were six different kinds of sandwiches: egg mayonnaise; chicken; prawn; banana and cream cheese; bacon, lettuce and tomato; and peanut butter and grape jelly. There were six different kinds of cake too: alphabet fairy cakes; chocolate crispies; chocolate fudge cake; blackcurrant cheese-cake; carrot cake and the special ginormous swimming-pool birthday cake. It had five marzipan girls in swimming costumes standing in the middle.

It was the most special birthday cake in the world.

DAISY
Sleepovers

It was Grandma and Grandpa's Pearl Wedding Anniversary in a couple of weeks.

'We're not having a party,' said Grandma. 'That's not our way.' She spoke as if parties were incredibly vulgar, on a par with naked mud wrestling in pig sties. 'We thought we'd like to celebrate the occasion with a special Sunday lunch.' She paused. 'Just for the family.'

She meant Jo and me. Once she was off the phone we moaned and groaned, trying to think up wild excuses to get out of it. We don't like going to Grandma and Grandpa's at the best of times.

CHARLIE
The Lottie Project

My Special Occasions

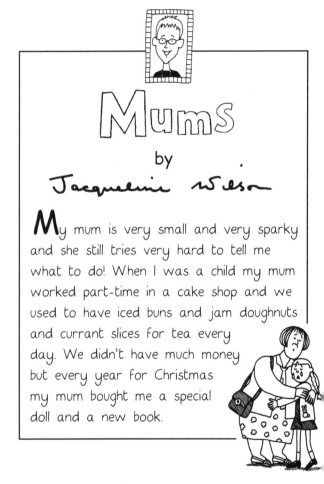

Mums

by

Jacqueline Wilson

My mum is very small and very sparky and she still tries very hard to tell me what to do! When I was a child my mum worked part-time in a cake shop and we used to have iced buns and jam doughnuts and currant slices for tea every day. We didn't have much money but every year for Christmas my mum bought me a special doll and a new book.

I loved being a mum myself. My daughter Emma and I played endlessly with *her* dolls and we read stories to each other and made up our own imaginary games. Emma loved playing Victorians. She was always a grand beautiful Victorian lady called Miss Emma and I would be her maid and had to curtsey to her and do as I was told!

Mum and I used to have lovely fun Sundays when we were just a family of two. We'd lie in bed late and play Bears-in-Caves under the bedcovers and once Mum let me take a jar of honey to bed with us and she just laughed when the sheets got all sticky. Mum liked reading the newspapers all morning. I liked drawing on the papers, giving all the ladies in the photos moustaches and the men long dangly earrings. Then we'd have a picnic lunch in the park. We even had picnics when it was raining. We didn't care. We just said it was lovely weather for ducks and went, 'Quack quack quack'.

LIZZY
Lizzy Zipmouth

Marigold was on her best behaviour all week. She didn't drink at all. She didn't swear or shout at anyone, she didn't go on a wild spending spree, she didn't stay in bed till lunchtime and stay up all night. She wore her mumsie jeans-and-T-shirt outfit and she made sure we had a proper tea every afternoon, baked beans on toast, sausage and chips, fish fingers, macaroni cheese.

DOLPHIN
The Illustrated Mum

Mum went after lots of jobs that summer but for a long time she kept getting turned down. She got very depressed and she even started getting thinner because she didn't feel like eating much. I'd always longed for Mum to stop being so fat, but now I wasn't sure. It was as if the Mum I knew was slowly wearing away, like a bar of soap. I wanted her really big and really bossy again, because that was the way she was supposed to be.

MANDY
Bad Girls

Patricia Williams was my first mum, though she wasn't permanent. She took in foster kids. She'd been doing it for years, babies a speciality, so they took me out of hospital when I was a few days old and she looked after me until I was nearly one. I wonder if she remembers me? If only I could remember her! I've got an idea of her in my head, big and soft and smelling of toast and fresh ironing.

APRIL
Dustbin Baby

Mum didn't get mad at me and shout. She didn't say very much at all. She did a lot of that sitting on the bed and staring into space. Sometimes Mack could snap her out of it. Sometimes he couldn't. I hated to see Mum all sad and sulky like that. I tried telling her jokes to cheer her up a bit.

'Hey Mum, what's ten metres tall and green and sits in the corner?'

'Oh Elsa, please. Just leave me be.'

'The Incredible Sulk!'

ELSA
The Bed and Breakfast Star

Mum stayed lovely day after day. She didn't go for another job just yet. She said she'd wait until after her operation. We used up the last of the lottery money. Mum kept

treating us. Kendall had red ice lollies cut up in his cornflakes for breakfast and red ice lolly soup for his tea. She read him

Thomas the Tank Engine until she was hoarse. She took him swimming and let George take a dip too, though he reeked of chlorine for ages afterwards. Mum made me Cadbury's chocolate sandwiches for breakfast and Ribena cocktails for my tea. She did my hair in a different elaborate style every day and made me up properly so that I looked almost pretty.

LOLA ROSE
Lola Rose

Don't get me wrong. I love it here at Nan's and I don't ever, ever, ever want to go back home. It's just I started wondering why my mum doesn't want me back. Doesn't she even want to know how I'm getting on? Isn't she worried about my cut? Why didn't she want to wish me a happy new year? There were people ringing from the other side of the world. Couldn't my mum be bothered to ring from the other side of London?

TREASURE
Secrets

People are sometimes sorry for me because I haven't got a mum. Sophie once put her arms around me and said it must be so awful. I was bad then and made myself look so sad that Sophie would be specially sweet to me, but I really don't mind a bit not having a mum. I don't miss her because I never knew her. The only time *I* get upset is when we go to visit my mum's grave. It's very pretty, with a white headstone and the words *Beloved Wife and Daughter* in curly writing.

VERITY
The Cat Mummy

I let myself think properly about Cam. All the stuff we did together. Daft things. . . like we'd dance to *Top of the Pops* and we'd shout out silly answers to the quizzes and we'd invent all sorts of new rude funny things to happen in all the soaps. And at night Cam would always tuck me up and ruffle my hair. And if I got scared at night – a bad dream or something – I could always go and climb into her bed. She'd moan and go, 'Oh Tracy Fidget Bottom', but she'd still cuddle me close.

TRACY BEAKER
The Dare Game

Why can't she be here for me? Doesn't she even remember me on my birthday? Doesn't she ever wonder what I've turned out like? I've thought of her every day of my life. She doesn't care. She gave birth to me but she shoved me straight in that bin and hasn't given me a second thought since. What sort of mum could throw her baby away? Maybe she isn't worth finding.

APRIL
Dustbin Baby

She mostly didn't want to play, she just wanted to lie back and smoke her roll-ups and drink and watch telly and if I pestered her she'd yell at me or give me a shove or a smack. She'd really lose it sometimes, telling me it was all my fault, if I hadn't been born she'd be out with her mates having fun instead of stuck at home night after night with a boring little brat like me.

TREASURE
Secrets

I looked at her, my illustrated mum. I knew she really did love me and Star. We had a father each and maybe they'd be around for us and maybe they wouldn't – but we'd always have our mum, Marigold. It didn't matter if she was mad or bad. She belonged to us and we belonged to her. The three of us. Marigold and Star and Dolphin.

DOLPHIN
The Illustrated Mum

My Mum

Dads

Dads

by

Jacqueline Wilson

I had a rather scary dad who lost his temper a lot so I didn't always feel very relaxed in his company. But he could sometimes be a great dad too. He read to me when I was little, though his choice of reading matter varied enormously. One day it could be the *Tupenny and Squibbet* children's comic strip from his evening paper, the next it could be a couple of chapters from *David Copperfield*.

He took me for long walks in the country too. We'd hike all day in the hills and lanes of Surrey. I liked a place called Silent Pool best, a lovely secret pool of very clear green water. There was a little ornamental hut there and I always wished I could live in it.

I was always on Dad's side no matter what. I love my mum but she's not *Dad*. Dad looks like a film star, he really does, with lovely blond hair and deep blue eyes and he's really fit too because he works out and plays a lot of sport. That was what Mum and Dad rowed about. Dad always flirted with all the ladies he met at badminton and tennis and swimming.

SAMANTHA
The Worry Website

Vicky's never understood what it's like with my dad. He can always get mad. I don't know if it's because he works nights. He usually leaves me alone but sometimes he can get really niggly, picking on me for the slightest thing. He can go crazy, yelling all sorts of stuff, waving his arms around, his fists clenched. He's never hit Mum or me but sometimes he hits the cushions or the sofa. One time he hit the kitchen wall and made the plaster flake. His knuckles bled but he didn't seem to notice.

JADE
Vicky Angel

Mum was so so so stupid when it came to dealing with Dad. She'd do anything for him, give him anything, do exactly what he said. It was partly because he was scared of him. But it was also because she was

still crazy about him. He's so good-looking, my dad, lean and tall, with deep blue eyes and a great tangle of black, wavy hair. Everyone thinks he looks incredible it's not just us. Lots of the women on our estate were nuts about him. Even some of the girls at school acted like he was a rock star.

LOLA ROSE
Lola Rose

I went swimming with Dad on Sunday and we had a great time. Dad showed me how to kick out my legs like a little frog and I swam ever such a long way without putting my foot down once. Then we played jumping up and down and then Dad pretended he was a dolphin and I rode on his back.

I really love my dad. He's a managing director of this big engineering firm, Major Products. I don't really know what major things they produce. I don't even know exactly what my dad does. He manages, he directs. He's always been a whizz at his job but now he acts like he's worried all the time. I tried massaging his neck for him yesterday but he pushed my hands away and said, 'Stop dabbing at me, India.'

INDIA
Secrets

I hate stepdads. I've got a real dad but I don't see him now. He stopped living with us ages ago. He doesn't come to see me but I don't care any more. My first stepdad doesn't come to see us either and I'm very, very glad about that. He was a scary monster stepdad. He pretended to be jolly and friendly at first. He bought me heaps of presents. He even bought me a Flying Barbie. I always badly wanted a Barbie doll but Mum never bought me one. She thinks they're too girly. I *like* girly things. I loved my Flying Barbie but I didn't ever love my first stepdad, even at the beginning.

LIZZIE
Lizzie Zipmouth

Laura's got a step*dad* and she certainly doesn't think much of him. He's the one who put poor Dustbin on a diet. He even suggested Laura's *mum* should go on a diet and made her upset about having a big bottom – which she can't help. Thank goodness Dad doesn't seem interested in any ladies, with big or little bottoms. He hardly ever talks about Mum but he once said she was the loveliest woman in the whole world and no one could ever replace her. This was a great relief.

VERITY
The Cat Mummy

I wished I'd been born part of Harpreet's family. I wished Harpreet's dad was *my* dad. I loved the way he put his arm around Harpreet and cuddled her close and called her his little girl. My dad had done all that with me. He called me all sorts of special things when he was in a good mood. I was his Princess Rosycheeks, his  Fairy Doll, his Jay-Jay Jam Doughnut. But the good mood could change to bad, and then he'd call me other stuff, short, sharp, ugly words that stuck to me like slime.

LOLA ROSE
Lola Rose

My Dad

Brothers and Sisters

Brothers and Sisters

by
Jacqueline Wilson

I was an only child but I longed for lots of brothers and sisters. I often wrote about very big families when I was little. I thought it would be much more fun to be part of a large family. I've still got one of these stories, about seven siblings. I included a pair of identical twins – and when I was grown up I very much enjoyed writing my book *Double Act* about the Barker twins, Ruby and Garnet. I've always been fascinated by identical twins. It must be so strange seeing someone who looks exactly the same as you, and it must be great growing up together, always having someone to play with and share secrets. Still, I'm not sure I'd like to have someone as fierce and bossy as Ruby as my twin!

I've been almost like Hannah's mum. When she was a baby I fed her and washed her and dressed her and changed her (yucky, but you have to do it). I cuddled her lots and played peek-a-boo and do you know something? The very first word she said was Holly. That's my name.

HOLLY
The Worry Website

Will wasn't even at school yet but he made up plays that lasted for hours. No, not hours – and they can't have been real plays. He just made Big and Little Growl dance about in front of me, one of them booming in a glorious great growl, one of them squeaking in a winsome weeny growl. I know that's all it can have been, and yet the carpet around me sprouted forests and Big Growl and Little Growl padded about me on real paws.

VIOLET
Midnight

I'm the one who had her work cut out coping with Kenny. I'd sneak over to the babies' playground to find Kenny trailing about by himself, head drooping. The other little kids would push him over just for the fun of it, leaving him snivelling, rubbing his eyes with his grazed hands, blood trickling down into his socks. He'd scream if the teachers or the dinner ladies went near him. I was the one who had to pick him up and mop him.

LOLA ROSE
Lola Rose

We'd got it all sorted out. We'd stick together when we were young

and when we were old

and when we were even older

and if we ever wanted to get married then we'd marry twins

and have twin babies

GARNET
Double Act

I certainly hate my sister Sarah-Jane. She is only a year younger than me but she's little and dinky-looking and she talks in a special lispy baby voice so that everyone treats her like she's five years old. It's so irritating having a *little* sister. She's allowed to kick me or elbow me in the rib and creep up behind me and pinch my neck but if I clump her one I'm in serious trouble. I'm *generally* in serious trouble at home about Sarah-Jane.

GREG
The Worry Website

Z is for Zoë

Carrie gave birth to my half-sister a week after Christmas. She should have hurried things up a bit so that she arrived on the proper present day but that's typical of Carrie, she's late for everything. . . I looked down at Zoë. She looked up at me. She had big blue eyes but her hair wasn't fair like Carrie and Crystal and Zen. She had toffee-coloured curls. She was going to be dark like Dad. Muddy-brown like me. I gently touched her starfish hand and her tiny fingers closed around my thumb.

ANDY
The Suitcase Kid

Hank got so good at crawling he could probably win a gold medal at the Baby Olympics. If we wanted any peace at all we had to change his crawling track into an obstacle race. Sometimes we collected several babies and had a proper race. The other brothers and sisters placed bets. That was good. Pippa and I coined it in, because Hank always won.

ELSA
The Bed and Breakfast Star

'You're two separate people who just happen to be sisters, aren't you? Garnet and Ruby. Or Ruby and Garnet. Whichever I've got muddled.'

'We like being called Twin,' I told her.

'That's what they call us at school,' said Garnet

'We are twins' I said.

'So we like' said Garnet.

'Being called' I said.

'Twins,' we said simultaneously.

RUBY
Double Act

My Brothers
and Sisters

Style

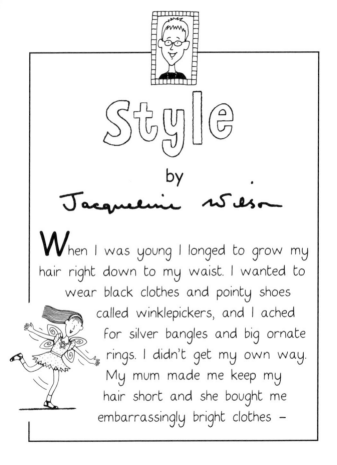

Style

by

Jacqueline Wilson

When I was young I longed to grow my hair right down to my waist. I wanted to wear black clothes and pointy shoes called winklepickers, and I ached for silver bangles and big ornate rings. I didn't get my own way. My mum made me keep my hair short and she bought me embarrassingly bright clothes –

shocking-pink jumpers, canary-yellow jackets, swimming-pool turquoise trousers. My shoes were depressingly sensible, with round toes and squat heels. My jewellery box contained a tiny pearl necklace and a weeny gold heart on a fragile chain. Now I can wear whatever I want! I wear black with witchy boots, my arms clank with bangles, and I wear a huge ring on every single finger. I still haven't managed to grow my hair though!

Mum wanted me to wear a proper long frilly bridesmaid's frock but it looked ever so silly on me. My hair still sticks out all over the place like a lion's mane and my legs are so skinny my socks always wrinkle and somehow they always get dirty marks all over them and my shoes go all scuffed at the toes right from when they're new. Mum sighed and said I'd get my frock filthy before she'd had time to get up and down the aisle.

ELSA
The Bed and Breakfast Star

I'd mucked about with make-up before, putting glitter on my eyelids and gloss on my lips, but I'd always wiped it off when Dad was due home. He said he didn't like to see his little girl all tarted up. I could paint on make-up an inch thick now. I attempted that special putting-on-lipstick smile but I got red all over my teeth, so I invented my own method, going slightly over the edge of my lips to make them look more voluptuous. I hoped I looked much older.

LOLA ROSE
Lola Rose

She was standing at the front, by Mrs Mason's desk, wearing her own clothes instead of our brown school uniform. They were amazing clothes too, a tiny black lace top, a silver and white embroidered waistcoat, a purple velvet tiered skirt edged with crimson lace, and black pointy Goth boots with high heels. She had brightly coloured Indian bangles jingling all the way up both arms and beads plaited into her hair. And what hair! Long blonde fairy princess waves all the way down to her waist.

VIOLET
Midnight

Gran made all our clothes too. That was *awful*. It was bad enough Gran being old-fashioned and making us have our hair in plaits. But our clothes made us a laughing stock at school, though some of the mums said we looked a picture. We had frilly frocks in summer and dinky pleated skirts in winter, and Gran knitted too – angora boleros that made us itch, and matching jumpers and cardis for the cold. Twinsets. And a right silly set of twins we looked too.

RUBY
Double Act

I wondered if Lily wished she could wear tiny T-shirts and embroidered jeans. Lily mostly worse big towelling tops because she dribbled and spilt so much and they stopped her getting too wet. She wore loose jogging trousers because they were easy to whip on and off when she needed changing. Lily's clothes were practical but they weren't *pretty*.

DAISY
Sleepovers

If I touched a special stud on my mattress I hurtled forwards ten years and grew willowy and beautiful with long thick hair down to my waist. Not fair like Star. Red like Marigold? No, as I got older my mousey hair would darken and I'd be raven black at twenty, with my own green eyes outlined with sooty lashes. I'd have clear white skin with just one exquisite tattoo on my shoulder, a little black witch. I'd have a nose stud too, emerald to match my eyes.

DOLPHIN
The Illustrated Mum

My Style

Pets

Pets

by

Jacqueline Wilson

I badly wanted a dog when I was growing up, but we lived in a council flat and pets weren't allowed. Well, I suppose I could have had a budgie or a goldfish, but I wanted a pet I could cuddle and take for walks. I spent hours playing with my friends' dogs, I collected little china poodles, and I had a toy Pekinese that I pretended was real.

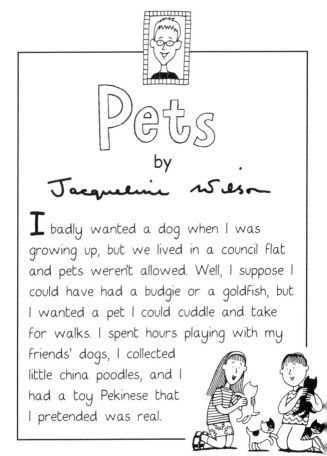

I still don't have a dog now. I travel around so much that it simply wouldn't be possible. But I'm planning on getting a dog in the future. It will have to be a *little* dog because my house is so cluttered up with thousands of books. I rather fancy a miniature black poodle. I'd like a cat too, a delicate Siamese with blue eyes.

My favourite animals are lemurs. They look so demure but if they're angry they can shriek alarmingly. They love the sun and bask on their backs with their arms spread out, just like little sunbathing people. They cuddle up close when they go to sleep, their tails coiled round in a ring.

Sporty

Scary

Baby

Posh

Dustbin

Licky

Crusher

Mabel

My best friend Sophie had got four kittens called Sporty, Scary, Baby and Posh. My second-best friend Laura has a golden Labrador dog called Dustbin. My sort-of-boyfriend Aaron has got a dog too, a black mongrel called Liquorice Allsorts, though he gets called Licky for short. My worst enemy Moyra has got a boa constrictor snake called Crusher. Well, she says she has. I've never been to her house so I don't know if she's telling fibs.

VERITY
The Cat Mummy

Kenny suddenly wailed that he wanted to take Bubble, our goldfish. I promised him he could have a whole tank of fish in our new place but Kenny wouldn't be diverted. He started howling, his arms around Bubble's bowl.

'Oh God, what next?' said Mum. She poured some water into a polythene bag and tipped Bubble into it. 'OK, he's coming too', she said.

I have a pet. She is a tabby cat called Mabel. I loved her dearly. But she is very, very, very *boring*. She doesn't do anything. She just sleeps. Sometimes I leave her curled up on my bed when I go to school and when I come home there she still is, in exactly the same position. She doesn't go out at night and run around having wild encounters with big bad tom cats. Not my Mabel.

VERITY
The Cat Mummy

Well, there's a rabbit called Lettuce at this home but it's a bit limp, like it's name. It doesn't sit up and give you a friendly lick like a dog. I think I'd like a Rottweiler and then all my enemies had better WATCH OUT.

TRACY BEAKER
The Story of Tracy Beaker

My Pets

Fears

Fears

by

Jacqueline Wilson

I used to have horrible nightmares when I was little. I was generally lost and someone was chasing me and they were getting closer and closer. I knew I was dreaming and I'd try desperately hard to open my eyes. Sometimes I'd *think* I was awake and I'd certainly be back in my own bed but then the nightmare monster would burst out of my wardrobe or leap through my window.

Luckily I don't often have nightmares now. I don't have any real fears, I just fuss about silly boring things like the dripping noise coming from my water tank and my moody computer printer that scores black lines through things when it's having a bad day.

I'm scared of sleeping because every time I start to dream Terry jumps out at me and he's whirling that belt, going *crack crack crack* with it like a whip. I wake with such a start and each time I tell myself it's OK, it's just a bad dream but then I remember Terry isn't a dream, he's real, and he's coming to get me. He's acting all soft and sweet like he really loves me and wants me back but I know just what will happen once he gets me behind closed doors.

TREASURE
Secrets

It's OK on the computer because it does a wiggly red line under the word if you've spelt it wrong. Almost every word I type ends up with wiggly red lines. I feel as if I am all wrong and there is a wiggly red line under me. I am bottom in the class. I am useless at everything. I can't add up or take away or multiply or divide. I can't make up stories. I can't remember History or Geography. I can't do IT. I can't draw.

WILLIAM
The Worry Website

I watched them, and every single time they swam past my heart thumped and sweat sprang out on my forehead. I felt sick, I needed the toilet, I couldn't stop shaking – but I stayed there. I counted each second until I got to three thousand six hundred. Then I moved. I'd endured the hour-long torture of the shark tank. This was a sign that I had completed my task. I had shown the Voice of Doom. Mum was going to get better.

LOLA ROSE
Lola Rose

The flat seemed so quiet without her. I wondered about playing some of Marigold's old tapes. But I didn't really want to think about Marigold or else I'd start worrying. I was worrying anyway. I kept looking all round the room, especially behind me. I kept feeling some crazy man was creeping up on me. Or some huge hairy spider was about to crawl on my foot. I pushed my chair right against the wall and tucked my legs up but it didn't make me feel any better.

DOLPHIN
The Illustrated Mum

My Fears

Wishes

Wishes

by

Jacqueline Wilson

I like making wishes. I always wish when I cut a slice of my birthday cake, I always wish on the first star I see in the sky at night, and I pull the wishbone in the turkey every Christmas. I make a wish

every time I make a trip to places that are very special to me – the top of a very high hill, an

ancient country church with beautiful
statues, a kissing stile at the end of a
long grassy track. I'm not going to tell
you what I wish for, because then my
wishes might not come true.

I used to make the same wish over and
over again when I was a child. I wished
that I could be a writer when I grew up
and get lots of books published. That wish
really did come true!

Then we all said what we wanted to be when we grew up. Emily said she wanted to be a footballer and if she couldn't she'd teach PE and I said I wanted to be an artist but if I couldn't I'd teach Art in school. Chloe said I was a useless copycat which wasn't fair because I've always loved Art and I'm good at teaching too. I teach Lily lots, even though she doesn't learn very quickly. Chloe said teachers were boring anyway and *she* was going to be a famous actress. Amy said she was going to be a famous dancer and Bella said she was going to be a famous TV chef.

DAISY
Sleepovers

Boyfriends are Big Trouble. You don't need them. But babies are lovely. I'm going to have lots when I'm old enough. I told Nan and she laughed.

'Steady on. You're the bright one of the family, Treasure. Don't you want to go on to university, be a career girl, eh?'

'I could be a mum *and* a career girl,' I said.

'That's it, Treasure, think big,' said Nan.

TREASURE
Secrets

If I was older I would live in this really great modern house all on my own, and I'd have my own huge bedroom with all my own things, special bunk beds just for me so that I'd always get the top one and a Mickey Mouse alarm clock like Justine's and my own giant set of poster paints and I'd have some felt tips as well and no one would ever borrow them and mess them up and I'd have my own television and choose exactly what programmes I want, and I'd stay up till gone twelve every night and I'd eat at McDonald's every single day and I'd have a big fast car so I could whiz off and visit my mum whenever I wanted.

TRACY BEAKER
The Story of Tracy Beaker

Ever since I was little I've wanted to be an actress. I know it's mad. I'm not anyone special. No one from our estate ever gets to do anything glamorous or famous, and anyway, even the richest, prettiest, most talented kids can't make a living out of acting. But I just want to act so *much*. I've never been in anything at all, apart from school stuff. I was an angel in the Nativity play way back in Year Two. Vicky got to be Mary.

JADE
Vicky Angel

If I ever win the lottery I'm going to buy a great big house – maybe one like this and it'll just be for really *special* people. Nan. India, if she wants. Patsy. Loretta and little Britney. Maybe Willie can hang out with us too. My mum can come, but only if she promises not to bring any blokes with her. Especially not Terry. It'll be my house and my rules and the minute anyone hits or gets drunk or shoots up they're *out*, no arguments, immediate eviction.

TREASURE
Secrets

I wrote her a little story about myself all right. I wrote that my real name is Elsarina and I'm a child star – actress, singer and comedienne – and I've been in lots of adverts on the telly and done panto and heaps of musicals, and I was actually currently starring in a travelling repertory

performance of *Annie* – me playing Annie, of course. And I wrote that my mum and the rest of the family were all in showbiz too, part of the company, and *that's* why we're currently living in a hotel, because we travel around putting on shows.

ELSA
The Bed and Breakfast Star

I'd have my own magical hair salon where I'd invent wonderful exotic styles for very special people. I'd adorn hair with flowers and little crystals and beadwork. I'd dye it fantasy shades of purple and turquoise and sky blue, I'd cut and colour and crimp all day while models and rock stars and fashion editors fawned all over me and famous photographers recorded my creations. Then I'd go home to my beautiful stylish designer flat, silver and black with a

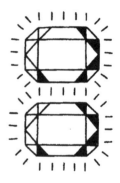

mirror ball revolving in each ceiling so that sparkles of light glimmered in every room. Star and Marigold would be there, desperate to please me.

DOLPHIN
The Illustrated Mum

If I could only earn my own money I could buy all the stuff I really need. It's not fair that kids aren't allowed to work. I'd be great flogging stuff down the market or selling ice creams or working in a nursery. If I could only get a job I could eat Big Macs and french fries every day and wear designer from top to toe, yeah, especially my footwear, and buy all the videos and computer games I want and take trips to Disneyland. Yeah! I bet my mum will take me to Disneyland if I ask her. It *is* going to end up like a fairy story. I'm going to live happily ever after.

TRACY BEAKER
The Dare Game

My Wishes

ABOUT THE AUTHOR

JACQUELINE WILSON was born in Bath in 1945, but has spent most of her life in Kingston-on-Thames, Surrey. She always wanted to be a writer and wrote her first 'novel' when she was nine, filling countless Woolworths' exercise books as she grew up. She started work at a publishing company and then went on to work as a journalist on *Jackie* magazine (which was named after her) before turning to writing fiction full-time.

Since 1990 Jacqueline has written prolifically for children and been awarded many of the UK's top awards for children's books, including the Smarties Prize in 2000 and the Guardian Children's Fiction Award and the Children's Book of the Year in 1999. Jacqueline was awarded an OBE in the Queen's Birthday Honours list, in Golden Jubilee Year, 2002.

Over 20 million copies of Jacqueline's books have now been sold in the UK and approximately 50,000 copies of her books are sold each month. An avid reader herself, Jacqueline has a personal collection of more than 15,000 books.

She lives in Surrey and has one grown-up daughter.

'A brilliant writer of wit and subtlety whose stories are never patronising and are often complex and many-layered' *The Times*